This book is being given to:

_____

On this date of:

_____

From:

_____

Message:

_____

Something's Eating the Garden

written and illustrated By
Pam Fries

Have fun in
the garden with the
animals! Blessings!

Pam Fries

MIGHTY LION PRESS

Something's Eating the Garden
Written and compiled by Mighty Lion Press
Copyright © 2018 Pam Fries

Mighty Lion Press
434 John Jacobs Road, Port Angeles, WA 98362
www.mightylionpress.com
mightlionpress@gmail.com

Ordering Information:
Quantity sales. Special discounts are available on quantity purchases by corporations, associations, and others. For details, contact the publisher at the address above.

Hardbacks and soft covers printed and published exclusively for the author by IngramSpark and eBooks by KDP Publishing in the United States of America

Editing by John Fox and Karyn Kirouac
Book layout by Hynek Palatin
Book cover design by Indie Publishing Group

Hardback ISBN: 978-1-7329803-0-3
Softback ISBN: 978-1-7329803-1-0
eBook ISBN: 978-1-7329803-2-7

Library of Congress Control Number: 2018914548

This book is dedicated to "Papa", my husband of 36 years, who left this life on earth to be in the arms of Jesus not long before this publishing. He supported my goal of finishing the illustrations and publishing this book about him and Laci, our first grandchild. Now, his passion and love for gardening will live on forever in print. We miss you honey.

Next to all my dear family and friends, and coworkers especially my mom, who endured and prayed me through the process of producing this book. I also thank all the people I didn't really know, like the many cashiers and bank tellers, who willingly gave me an ear and endured me sharing the manuscript and pictures in anticipation of publishing.

Most of all to my Lord, Jesus Christ who has paved the way for this book at every twist and turn for the last 7 years. If I had known what was going to happen this year before starting this process, the book would have never been finished. You knew I would need a distraction and boy did you provide!

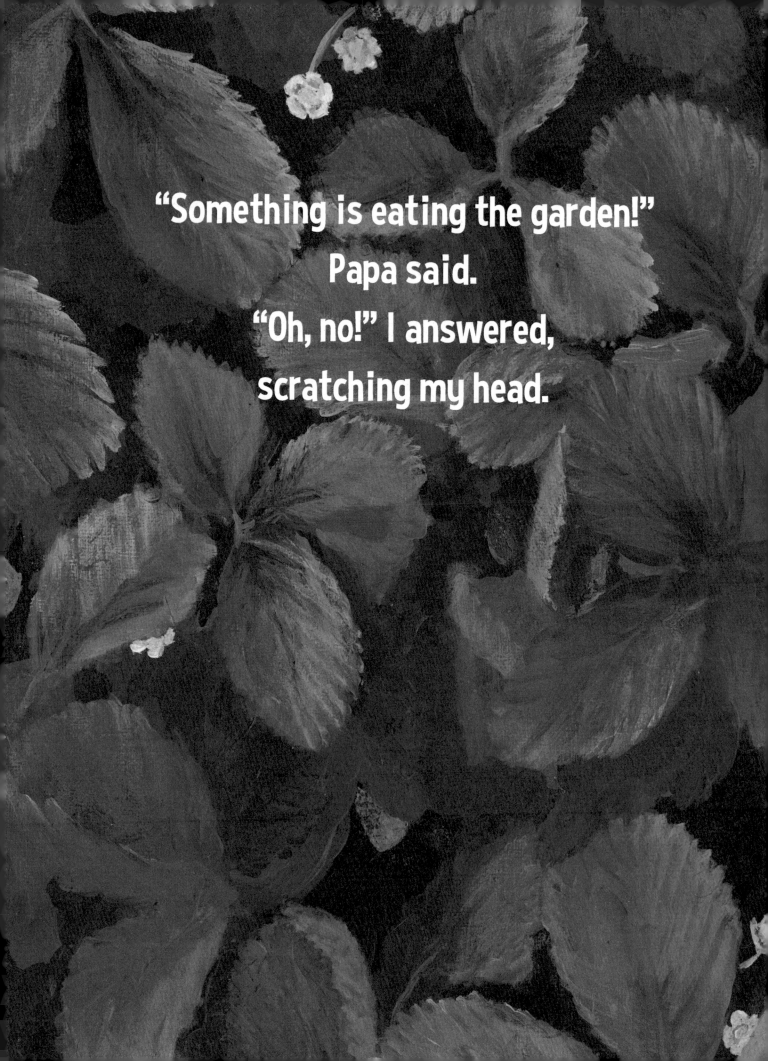

"Something is eating the garden!"
Papa said.
"Oh, no!" I answered,
scratching my head.

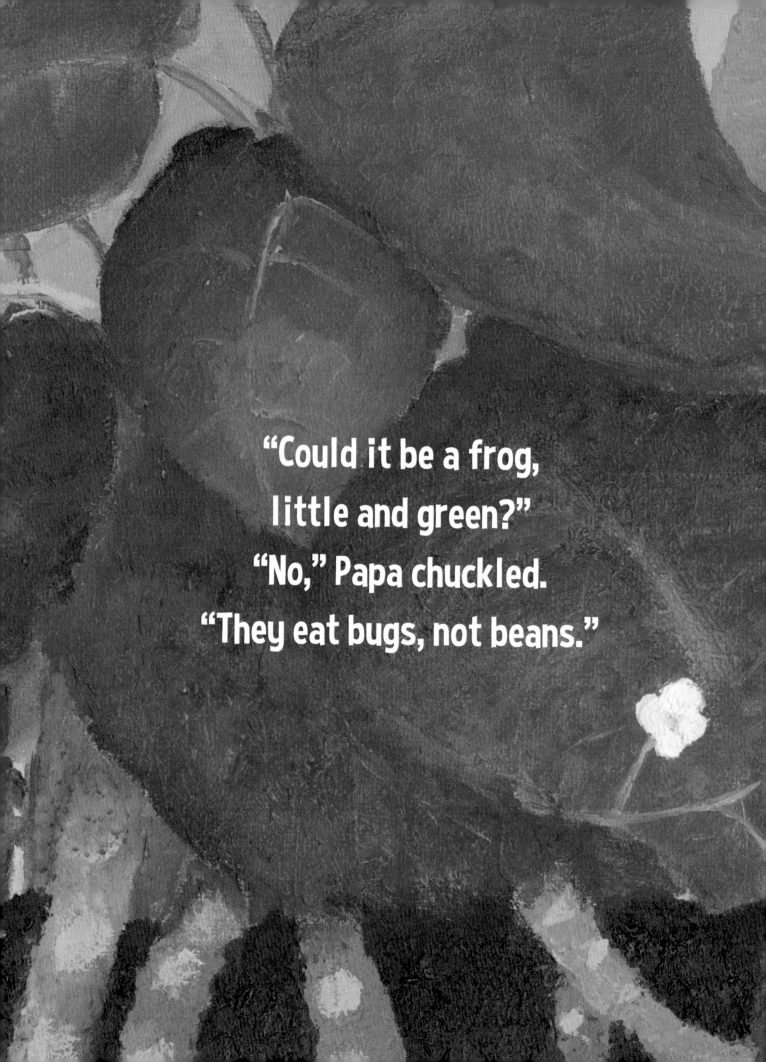

"Could it be a frog,
little and green?"
"No," Papa chuckled.
"They eat bugs, not beans."

"Maybe it's a sneaky
bandit raccoon
that comes and eats
by the light of the moon."

"Or a deer that nibbles off the tops of the big and beautiful vegetable crops."

"Or how about a tall,
spotted giraffe?"
"Nope, that's not it,"
Papa said with a laugh.

"Then it must be a bear
that is looking for honey?"

"It is smaller," said he,
"and it's not a bunny."

"Okay, then an elephant would be way too big."

"I know, I know,
it must be a pig!"

He shook his head
and said with a smile,
"It is not a pink pig,
nor a long crocodile!"

I sighed and said,
"I give up! What can it be?"

Then I looked at my plate...

and I knew it was ME!

The End

PAM FRIES, the author and illustrator, is also a mother and grandmother. Spending her time with her family and animals keeps her busy but her love for painting and drawing fills her spare time.

She chose the field of Primary Education in college. Then went on to teach preschool and substitute teach in grades Kindergarten through Middle School. After having children, she turned to homeschooling her own children for many years. She especially enjoyed the children's vivid imagination during the preschool years.

Something's Eating the Garden was inspired after a visit her husband and granddaughter, Laci, took to "Papa's" amazing garden many years ago.